The Brainstorm

For once I knew what my father meant when he called me Hurricane Elaine. Why had I jumped so quickly to baby-sit for Monsieur DuBois? Well, it's hard to say no to someone when you are in love with them. And besides, I really had thought I was accepting a date with him when I said I was free Saturday. Somehow I had to tell either Scott or Monsieur DuBois that I wasn't really free on Saturday. Then I had a brainstorm. . . .

HURRICANE ELAINE

Johanna Hurwitz

AN
APPLE
PAPERBACK

SCHOLASTIC INC.
New York Toronto London Auckland Sydney

ISBN 0-590-40766-X

12 11 10 9 8 7 6 5 4 3 2 1   8 9/8 0 1 2 3/9

Printed in the U.S.A.   01

First Scholastic printing, February 1988

For Louise, David, Amy, Mara, Heather, and Erica Fox — good friends through every kind of weather.

1. Peabody and Poughkeepsie

At six-thirty this morning, my alarm clock jolted me awake. I jumped out of bed half-asleep and charged into the bathroom. I wanted to beat the rest of my family to the shower.

As the water hit my head, it dawned on me that this was Saturday. No wonder I was so tired. I had been baby-sitting until one o'clock last night, and I had forgotten to change the setting on my clock. So here I was half-awake and half-washed when I could still be snuggled under my covers. *Elaine Sossi, how could you be so stupid?* I said to myself and finished getting washed.

It wasn't even seven o'clock yet. Since I

had the bathroom to myself for a change, I decided to wash my peach-colored lamb's wool sweater. My best friend Sandy told me that if you wash sweaters with shampoo they come out extra soft. I washed it carefully using the very expensive shampoo that I had splurged on last week. Then I put some newspapers down on the desk and a towel over the newspapers and arranged my sweater to dry. I could see that Sandy was right about the shampoo. Even wet, the sweater looked good. It smelled good, too.

It was still too early for breakfast. If I waited long enough, I knew my mother would make French toast. So I removed the chipped nail polish that I was wearing and put on a fresh coat. By the time the polish dried, my mother was in the kitchen.

When I went downstairs, my brother Aldo was sitting at the kitchen table with Poughkeepsie on his lap. Poughkeepsie is one of our two cats. The other one is named Peabody.

"Don't tell me Poughkeepsie is going to have breakfast with us," I groaned.

"He's already eaten," said Aldo. "He's just keeping me company while I wait for the food."

Aldo is crazy about animals. He treats the cats like people. If Aldo had his way, our house would be filled with animals. But if I had my way, Peabody and Poughkeepsie would be given to another family first thing this morning. Who needs them?

"How many slices?" asked my mother as she started to make the French toast.

"Four," said Aldo.

"*Mon Dieu*," I gasped. "You are a pig." It annoys me that he can eat so much without gaining weight.

"You're lucky that I'm not an elephant," Aldo said. "Did you know that elephants eat sixteen hours a day?"

"You're making that up," I said as my mother put a slice of French toast on a plate for me.

"No, I'm not," Aldo insisted. "I learned it from a nature show on television."

"No wonder elephants look the way they do," my sister Karen giggled. She's going on fourteen, a year younger than I am, but the way she acts you'd think she was ten like Aldo.

My mother laughed and offered me another slice of French toast.

I was rescued from the temptation by a horn honking outside. That was Sandy Lorin and her mother. We go shopping at the flea market in Jefferson almost every Saturday. It's about a half-hour drive from here.

"See you all later," I called and charged out the door. As it slammed behind me, I remembered that I hadn't cleared my dishes from the table. It's a family rule, but I often forget.

At the flea market, Mrs. Lorin arranged where she would meet us, and then she went off in one direction, and Sandy and I went in another.

At the first table we passed I picked up a red plastic bracelet.

"Only two dollars," said the woman behind the table.

As I opened my pocketbook to get the money, Sandy gave me a push and said, "There are other tables with jewelry here."

Sandy likes to take her time and look around. She has saved me a lot of money this year. My father says I'm impulsive. That's why he calls me Hurricane Elaine. He says I do everything at ninety miles an hour. Sure enough, on the other side of the market, we found the same bracelet and it was only a dollar. The best thing about Sandy is that she never says, "I told you so."

We walked around examining T-shirts and shoes, but my only other purchase was a bottle of green nail polish.

All in all, it was a good morning. I didn't realize it was going to turn into such a lousy day.

Back home, I ran upstairs to put my bracelet and nail polish away in my bedroom. I saw right away that the sweater I had washed this morning was covered with paw prints. One of those horrible cats had taken a walk across my peach-colored lamb's wool sweater.

I charged downstairs and ran to my mother. "Do you know what one of those cats did?"

"It will wash out," she said when she heard what had happened.

"I already washed that sweater once today," I complained. "And I used my expensive shampoo, too."

"No one told you to spend all that money on shampoo," my mother said. "Next time use regular soap. I provide it free of charge."

"That's not the point," I said. "Those cats are into everything. And they leave cat hairs on all my clothes."

"Only on the clothing you leave lying around," my mother said. "If you hung up your things, you wouldn't have that problem."

"If we didn't have those cats, I wouldn't have any problems," I fumed.

At the moment, Karen came out to tell us that lunch was ready. My sister thinks a terrific way to spend a Saturday is cooking in the kitchen. I'm not complaining because everything she makes is good. Still it is a peculiar way for a girl her age to act.

In the middle of eating Karen's eggplant

casserole, my left ankle started to itch. I tried rubbing it with my right ankle. That didn't help. I reached under the table to scratch. Then my right ankle began to itch.

"Elaine, what in the world are you doing?" my mother asked.

"I have a terrible itch," I complained. I pushed back my chair. Both of my ankles were covered with tiny red spots.

"Can't be chicken pox," I said. "I already had that."

"I have the same thing," said Aldo as he pulled up his sleeves to show off his spots.

"Maybe it's poison ivy," Karen suggested.

"I think I have it, too," my mother said.

"It's an epidemic!" I groaned.

"No, it's not," my father said. "I bet Peabody and Poughkeepsie have fleas. You must all have flea bites."

"Those cats have got to go," I shuddered. "I won't live in a house full of bugs."

"It's a good thing we didn't feel that way when you got head lice in second grade," my mother joked.

"I never had head lice."

"You certainly did. Every single child in Mrs. Frazier's second-grade class at P.S. 35 had head lice that year. I cut your hair short and shampooed it with a special solution — it was *very* expensive," my mother added. "And I kept you. Even though I knew that Karen and Aldo and your father and I might catch your lice."

"That's not the point," I said. "What I want to know is what are you going to do with these cats of ours?"

"It's after one o'clock," Aldo pointed out. "The vet's office is closed."

"I'll call him first thing Monday morning," my mother promised.

Already I was feeling itchy all over, even where there were no flea bites. "I think we should just get rid of the cats and clean this place up once and for all."

"Calm down, Elaine," my father said. "We all want to get rid of the fleas. But a week from now, we'll be laughing at this."

That seemed very unlikely to me.

"Didn't anybody like my casserole?" Karen asked.

Who could eat now?

"Do you think it needed more cheese?"

"More cheese, less fleas," I said as I got up to phone Sandy. This time my mother called me back to clear my dishes from the table. I wondered if Sandy's family would like to adopt me.

"Can you believe it?" I told Sandy on the phone. "We have fleas."

"How did you get them?"

"It's an early Christmas present from Peabody and Poughkeepsie. Aldo is searching for some right now with a magnifying glass. He's probably going to try to make pets out of them."

"Oh, gross," Sandy said, when I heard my mother shouting up the stairs. "Time's up, Elaine."

Even if she doesn't want to make a call and she's not expecting one, my mother won't let me stay on the phone longer than five minutes.

One time, Sandy and I tried to get around her rule by having Sandy call me every five minutes. But my mother got furious. She said if I wanted to talk to Sandy I should just walk down the street.

Just because Sandy lives three houses away, my mother thinks it's silly for us to speak on the telephone. Why did Alexander Graham Bell go to all that trouble to invent the phone, for heaven's sake? On his first call, he spoke to a man in the next room. That's much closer than three houses away!

I don't know which is worse: having fleas or having a mother who clocks you every time you use the telephone. But there wasn't anything I could do about either.

"Gotta go," I sighed. *"Au revoir."*

I hung up the phone and started scratching. The only part of my body that didn't itch was my teeth.

2. Men and Boys

Having fleas at home makes you really love going to school. Actually, I have always liked school. But ever since I started taking French with Monsieur DuBois, I love school.

Monsieur DuBois speaks with a French accent. I could listen to him talking all day long. And he is very handsome. He has a moustache and a beard and it really makes him look sexy. All the girls have crushes on him. But I've got the best grades in the class, and I think he likes me the best.

Sometimes I can't help wondering what it would feel like to kiss Monsieur DuBois. (His first name is Pierre.) Would his beard and moustache tickle? I think I would die if he ever did kiss me.

Sandy is in French with me. I can't understand why some kids would want to study Spanish. The Spanish teacher is about eighty years old and she has dyed hair that looks like it belongs on a broom.

Monsieur DuBois returned the quizzes that we had last week. My paper had an *A* written on it in red ink and the words *très bien*. I treasure all my French papers because he's written on them. I even saved a piece of gold foil that was wrapped around a French candy that he distributed to us during an exam.

"I have an announcement," Monsieur DuBois said: "You have all worked diligently to learn French vocabulary. Now I think we should put it to use. A friend of mine is the owner of Le Petit Bistro. We can go there and have a French meal for ten dollars a person, if you can all afford that."

All around the room students turned to look at one another. Who had ever heard of going out to dinner with a teacher?

"One rule," said Monsieur DuBois when he saw that everyone liked his idea. "During the meal, no one can speak a single word of English."

"That's one way to keep us quiet," Evan Charles called out from the back of the room. He's good at making wisecracks in English, but he's not so clever in French.

When class was over, Sandy and I walked to our geometry class. "He sure is neat," Sandy sighed. "Imagine thinking of taking us all out to dinner."

"He's not exactly taking us if we have to pay for ourselves," said Scott Welles. Scott recently transferred to our school. He sits behind me in French. He also happens to be Sandy's cousin. He has blond hair and dimples and is quite good looking, as fifteen-year-old boys go. I prefer Monsieur DuBois's appearance myself.

"Have you ever eaten in a French restaurant?" I asked him.

"If a restaurant doesn't sell pizza, I'm not interested," Scott said.

"Won't you come with us?" Sandy asked.

"*Oui, oui,*" said Scott. "But promise

you'll let me sit next to you, Elaine. I don't want to order something horrible."

"I think he really likes you," Sandy said as Scott turned down the corridor toward his next class.

I didn't want to sit next to Scott at Le Petit Bistro. I hoped I could arrange to sit next to Monsieur DuBois.

"Scott's just afraid of getting horse meat. Remember Monsieur DuBois said you could get that in some French restaurants?"

"Gross," Sandy shuddered as we walked into geometry. That's the way I feel about geometry. Gross.

That same day in the cafeteria, Scott Welles gave me an apple. Well, he didn't exactly *give* it to me. He threw it at me. Sandy and I were standing on the lunch line. Scott was ahead of us. After he picked up his food, he turned around. "Do you want this?" he called. Suddenly an apple was flying toward me. By some miracle, I managed to catch it.

"Not bad," Scott called as he walked off to join his friends across the room.

"See," said Sandy. "He really likes you."

I bit into the apple. It wasn't something I was going to keep forever like the gold foil from Monsieur DuBois's candy.

"He's not my type," I said and took another bite of the apple.

"But he's not ancient like Monsieur DuBois. You can't marry a man who is old enough to be your father."

"I'm not marrying anybody," I protested. But I felt my face turning red. Monsieur DuBois isn't *that* old. I figured out that he must be about twenty-eight.

"Tomorrow is Flower Day," Sandy reminded me as we finished our lunch.

"How could I forget with the signs all over the school?"

"Why don't you send a carnation to Scott?" Sandy suggested. Every year the Student Council holds a fund-raising sale. White, pink, and red carnations are sold for a dollar each, and the money goes to the school's cultural-arts fund.

Last year, Sandy bought a carnation for me, and I bought one for her. You pay for them, and then the flowers are delivered during the school day. It's exciting to be sitting in class and have a messenger come in and present you with a flower — even if you know it was your girlfriend and not a secret admirer who sent it. Last year Monsieur DuBois went home with a whole bouquet — more than any other teacher in the school.

"Will you?" Sandy nagged at me. "Will you send a flower to Scott?"

"I'll think about it," I said.

By the end of the day Sandy had talked me into sending a carnation to Scott. I wondered if he was planning to send one to me. After all, he'd have to pay for it. The apple had come with his lunch — for free.

When I got home from school, my mother had fumigated the house with flea bombs. What a terrible stink. I'd almost rather have fleas!

3. 347 Possibilities

The next morning, I got up extra early to dress. I put on the green cotton sweater that I bought last month. I had been saving it for a special occasion because it makes my eyes look green. I was wearing the green nail polish, too. It was almost the same shade as my sweater.

"Are you going out of the house like that?" Karen gasped when she saw me. "You could pass for a witch straight out of *Macbeth*."

Show off. I knew her English class had been reading that play.

"If you didn't bite your nails, I would lend you some of my polish," I offered.

"Green goes with a jealous personality."

"All right, girls," my mother said. "Finish your breakfasts before you miss the school bus."

Karen and I met Sandy at the bus stop.

"Do you have your money?" she asked, giving me a knowing wink.

"Yep," I said, patting my shoulder bag. "I'm all set to buy two flowers today."

Sandy grinned. "What colors are you going to buy? I'm going to get you a pink one. It will look good on your green sweater."

"Listen, Sandy," I said. "I can't afford to give you a flower this year. I'm getting one for Scott and one for Monsieur DuBois."

Just then the bus pulled up and we all piled on. I could see Sandy was disappointed. "Then I won't send you one either," she said as we sat down. "So don't expect to be carrying a bouquet when you come home this afternoon."

Sandy opened her science notebook and pretended to study. But I knew that she wasn't.

We got to school early so I had plenty of time to order the flowers I was sending. I chose red for Monsieur DuBois and pink for Scott. I had already decided that I would send my flowers without any messages.

On Tuesdays I have Earth Science class first period. Everyone calls it Advanced Chaos. Last week we tried to build a cloud in a jar. It didn't work. Once something we did created so much smoke that the school's alarm system went off and 350 students had to march out of the building in the pouring rain.

Ten minutes into first period, the door swung open and the first flowers of the day began to arrive. Mrs. Baron, our teacher, received a pair of pink carnations. Everyone knew who had sent them. Mr. Baron teaches math in our school. Soon other flowers were delivered. A girl named Laura got a red flower and a boy named Curtis got a white one. None were for me, but it was only first period. There were seven more to go.

All morning long Student Council members were running up and down the corridors making the deliveries. At lunch, I met Sandy at our usual table. I still hadn't gotten a flower. Then I saw Scott waiting on the hot-lunch line and he had a pink carnation stuck behind his ear.

"Maybe someone else sent him one, too," said Sandy.

Why was she being so mean? After all, it was her idea that I send Scott a flower. We hardly said a word to each other as we began to eat our lunches.

The flower squad was making deliveries in the cafeteria. Suddenly a boy from my English class was standing next to me. He looked at the tags on the flowers that he was holding and separated one from the bunch.

"Ta-dum," he sang as he pulled out a long green stem with no flower attached to it. He handed it to me and shrugged as if to say, it isn't my fault.

A stem without a flower costs only a quarter. Kids send them to teachers they don't like. Last year, Mr. Korman, the assistant principal, received a half-dozen.

It's a joke, but it's not a joke. It's awful.

I should have just dropped it on the floor. But, like an idiot, I sat there holding that stem.

"I suppose this is your idea of a joke," I said to Sandy. "What kind of a friend are you?"

"I didn't send it. Honest," Sandy said. "Look." She bent down and picked up a slip of paper that had fallen to the floor. "This came with the flower. I mean stem."

I grabbed the paper. "This makes me think of you."

It wasn't Sandy's handwriting. And it wasn't Karen's either. That left only 347 other possibilities in the school.

I looked at the narrow stem. "Whoever sent this doesn't think I need to lose weight," I said. "That's a small consolation." I bit into my sandwich and tried to pretend that I was amused.

A couple of girls from the next table came over. They had seen the delivery and wanted to admire my flower.

"Yikes," said Roseanne. "Who sent you a stem?"

"My secret admirer," I said. I was trying very hard to act as if I thought it was a wonderful joke.

And then, as if I wasn't feeling bad enough, who should walk over to our table but Scott Welles.

"Any flowers delivered over here?" he asked.

"None of your business," I snapped at him.

"What's wrong?" he asked, looking puzzled.

"Did you send any flowers to anyone today?" I asked him.

"It so happens that I did," he said, smiling.

If I had felt bad before, I felt even worse now. Scott had sent a flower to another girl. And Sandy had talked me into sending him a flower. Maybe she had already told Scott the pink carnation was from me. It was all I could do to keep from snatching it back.

"Who did you send a flower to?" Sandy asked.

"Someone you know very well. In fact,

she eats lunch with you every day," Scott grinned at us both.

I waved the stem in Scott's face. "If this is your idea of a joke, I don't think it's funny. You have a weird sense of humor." I had to get away, or I knew I would burst into tears. I don't think I have ever felt so embarrassed.

Scott looked at me as if I was crazy.

"There must be some mistake," said Sandy.

Just then the warning bell rang for the next period. I had never been so glad to get out of the lunchroom before.

I threw the stem and my uneaten sandwich into the garbage bin and ran all the way to geometry. For once, I was glad to be studying equilateral triangles. Anything was better than thinking of red, white, and pink carnations and stems without flowers attached.

4. Gone Wrong Day

I blame everything that happened that afternoon on the stem. If I had gotten a carnation from Scott, I would have come home from school feeling great. I would have put it in the bud vase that my Aunt Eleanor sent my mother for Christmas last year, and I would have looked at it while I conjugated French verbs and did geometry equations.

But I didn't have a flower and I was miserable. I had let Sandy convince me that Scott liked me and that I liked Scott, too. He didn't look anything like Monsieur DuBois. But he has a great smile and his blond hair and dimples are nice, too. Well, if a stem was his idea of a joke, it just showed how immature he was. No wonder I was attracted to older men like Pierre DuBois.

I kept my nose stuck in my French notebook all the way home. Sandy pointedly avoided me and talked to another girl on the bus. My green nail polish that I had put on that morning now reminded me of the green stem. I couldn't wait to get home and remove it.

When the bus reached our stop, I jumped off before Sandy and Karen. I wanted to escape into my room without having to talk to my sister who was holding a red carnation (probably from her friend Annette). And I was in no mood to talk to Sandy.

"Elaine." My mother called after me as I charged up the stairs.

I ran into my bedroom and dropped my school books. I had an unwanted guest. Poughkeepsie was sound asleep on my bed.

"Scat! Scat," I shouted, but he didn't budge. I picked him up. Any other time, removing the cat from my bed would have satisfied me. But that afternoon, I wanted to do more. I carried the cat all the way downstairs and opened the front door.

"Go take a long walk on a short dock," I shouted and slammed the door shut.

When we lived in Manhattan, Peabody and Poughkeepsie never went outside. But since we've moved to Woodside, the cats lead more adventurous lives. They are in and out of the house all day long. If they're not inside before he goes to bed, Aldo stands in the doorway, claps his hands, and they always come running.

I stomped back upstairs to my room and brushed off my bedspread. My mother had set off flea bombs, but there could be survivors.

I had just finished removing the green polish, when my mother called me again.

"What do you want?" I shouted.

"I need your help."

"I'm busy," I called back.

Just then the telephone rang, and I made a dash to answer it. My mother beat me to it by picking up the extension in the kitchen. I heard her say, "I'm sorry, Sandy. Elaine is very busy now and doesn't want to be interrupted." Then she hung up before I could say a word.

I charged down the stairs. "Why did you do that?"

"Why did you come home, if you won't greet anyone and won't answer me when I speak to you?" my mother said.

"I'm in a bad mood."

"So I noticed," my mother said. "But you do live in a house with other people. And I need you to help cut these string beans for supper."

"Where's Karen?" I asked. "Where's Aldo? Why do I have to be Cinderella around here?"

"Karen went to the store, and Aldo went over to DeDe's house after school. But even if they were both here, everyone has to take a turn helping in this family. And that means *you*, too."

"Can't I at least call Sandy first? It might be very important."

"It might be, but I doubt it. You can call her when you finish with the beans."

I started cutting.

"How was school?" my mother asked.

"Lousy."

"Anything you want to tell me about?" she asked.

"No."

"Karen gave me the carnation she got for Flower Day," my mother said finally. The bud vase with Karen's carnation in it was on the kitchen table. "Did you and Sandy exchange flowers this year?"

"No." I kept on cutting the beans with my head down. I didn't want to talk about it. "Here," I said handing her the pot of beans. "I'm going to call Sandy."

"Only five minutes," my mother reminded me. Wouldn't you think that just once she would give in and let me stay on the phone for six minutes?

I ran upstairs and dialed Sandy's number.

"Hi. What's up?" I asked her.

"I can't talk to you now. I'm busy," said Sandy coldly.

"What?"

"You're not the only one who is too busy to talk on the phone," she said.

"Hey come off it, Sandy," I said.

"I said I was busy," Sandy repeated. "Your mother told me that you were too busy to talk to me. Now I'm telling you that I'm too busy to talk to *you*." I heard the click of the phone as Sandy hung up on me.

I stood for a moment with the telephone receiver in my hand. I could not believe how many things had gone wrong today. I stood there wondering, should I call her back again or what? Ever since we moved to Woodside, Sandy has been my best friend. But today — first she gets angry with me because I didn't give her a carnation, then her stupid cousin pulls that prank on me and she doesn't even take my side. And now this. Well, if that is the way she feels, so be it. I don't need her friendship.

I was still holding the phone when I heard the screeching of car brakes out on the street. I ran to the window to look out. Mr. Lorin, Sandy's father, was standing in the street by his car. Doors were opening and people were coming out to see what had happened.

My mother had already gone outside,

too. I ran out and pushed my way through the crowd. There was something on the ground. I moved closer. Lying in the road with blood coming out of his mouth was our cat Poughkeepsie.

5. Part of Our Family

I turned and ran back to my house.

Karen was standing in the doorway holding a bag of groceries.

"There's been an accident," I said. "Poughkeepsie was hit by a car. I think he's dead."

Right at that moment, Aldo came riding down the street on his bike. Before I could stop him, I heard his cry. Aldo dropped his bike on the ground. He looked at Mr. Lorin accusingly. "You didn't have to hit him. You shouldn't have hit him!"

"It was an accident, Aldo," said Mr. Lorin. "There was no way I could have avoided the cat. It all happened too fast."

"You weren't to blame," my mother said. "The cats do run into the street."

I felt a hand on my arm. "Elaine. I'm sorry."

It was Sandy. At that moment, it didn't matter if she was sorry for our fight or sorry about Poughkeepsie. I just wanted to hug her.

"It wasn't your father's fault," I said. I knew I was just as guilty as Mr. Lorin. I was the one who had thrown the cat out this afternoon.

The crowd began to break up. It was suppertime, and people went home to eat. I don't remember who it was, but someone picked up Poughkeepsie and put him into a large box.

My mother put her arm around Aldo and steered him inside. Karen and I followed.

"I'll talk to you later," said Sandy, standing with her father. Mr. Lorin looked pale.

Supper was forgotten. We just sat around in the living room. My father came in from work and we told him what had happened.

"Aldo is taking this real bad," said Karen.

"We all feel bad," said my mother. "After all, Poughkeepsie was part of our family."

"If we still lived in the city, this wouldn't have happened," Aldo sobbed. "In the city the cats never went outdoors."

"Poughkeepsie was eleven years old," my father reminded him.

"Seventy-seven," said Karen. "Every year for a cat is equal to seven years for a human being."

"*C'est très bien*," I said. "That's a very good age for a cat."

"You're probably glad he's dead," Aldo shouted at me. "You didn't like him anyhow. You said we should get rid of both cats. Well, now you don't have to worry about the fleas."

"We still have Peabody and his fleas to keep us company," I shouted back.

My mother put her arms around Aldo. "No matter what she said, Elaine isn't responsible for Poughkeepsie's death," she said. "It was an accident. It could have happened any day of the week."

I opened my mouth to say something and then closed it again. No one in the family knew that I *was* responsible. But admitting it would not bring back Poughkeepsie. It would just make Aldo feel worse.

"Where is Peabody?" cried Aldo, jumping up.

"He's still outside," Karen said.

"We have to bring him in." Aldo ran to the door and began clapping his hands.

In a minute, Aldo returned with Peabody in his arms. "I'm never letting him go outside again," he announced, burying his face in the cat's fur.

"Now wait a minute," my father said. "We could have kept the cats locked up. But the freedom they had gave Poughkeepsie and Peabody a great deal of pleasure."

"Remember how they liked to roll in the grass?" said Karen. "In the city, they didn't even know there was such a thing as grass."

"Remember how they chased birds?" I offered and immediately wished I hadn't mentioned that. Me and my big mouth. Aldo always got upset when Peabody or Poughkeepsie brought a dead bird into the house.

"Do you know," my mother said gently, "that every time you go off on your bikes, I'm concerned about your safety? But what kind of life would you have if I didn't let you go off and do new things?"

It was quiet in the room except for Aldo's sniffling.

"Poughkeepsie had a good life. We are all sad because we loved him. Even with fleas, we loved him." My mother looked at me. "Try not to feel guilty because Poughkeepsie was killed. Feel sad, but not guilty."

"Maybe we could get a new cat," I suggested. Considering how I feel about cats, I guess I was still feeling guilty.

"I don't want a new cat. I want Poughkeepsie!" Aldo said. He sat stroking Peabody's fur. "Do you think he understands what happened?"

Watching Aldo petting the cat and whispering into its ear, I thought what a funny kid he was. Last summer, he ran about in the backyard and collected a whole jar full of fireflies. I remembered how he had brought the jar into the house and how the lid had accidentally come off. That night there was a pair of bugs flashing their little lights on and off in my bedroom. I complained about it the next morning, but the truth is that it was very funny. Who else has fireflies *inside* their home?

It was another hour before we sat down to eat. Despite the late hour, none of us had much appetite. The only one who seemed unconcerned about the tragic events of the afternoon was Peabody. He ate his supper with his usual gusto and then walked off. If he missed his companion, no one knew. When I returned to my bedroom later, I found Peabody lying on my bed. I didn't throw him off.

6. A Ghost in the House

The next morning, I felt like I should be dressed in black. The gloom around the kitchen table was thick.

"Can I stay home today?" Aldo begged my mother. "It doesn't seem right to go to school and do everyday things the morning after Poughkeepsie was killed."

"I'm sorry," my mother said. "I understand how you feel, but I really think it will be better for you to keep your mind occupied with school."

I was trying not to feel guilty. I told myself it was just a coincidence that the one day I threw Poughkeepsie out of the house the accident happened. But the sight of Aldo across from me at the breakfast table made me lose my appetite. It's hard to eat when someone sitting across from you is weeping into his orange juice.

"Poughkeepsie was like a brother to me," Aldo said miserably.

"We all loved him," my father said.

I put down my slice of toast. No matter what my mother said, I was at least partly responsible for Poughkeepsie's death.

I told Sandy how I felt about the accident as we rode to school. Because it was her father who had run over Poughkeepsie, I knew she'd understand. It was hard to remember that just yesterday we had quarreled.

"Why don't you get another cat?" Sandy asked.

"He says he doesn't want a new cat. He only wants Poughkeepsie."

"A cat is a cat," she said.

"*Un chat est un chat*," I repeated her words. I liked the way it sounded in French. "That's the way I feel, too. I guess it's because I'm not an animal lover like Aldo."

"You save your passion for something else," Sandy teased.

"Don't mention Scott Welles to me ever again," I warned. "You can't help it if he's your cousin, but he's a rat."

I realized that in a few minutes I would be seeing Scott. On Wednesdays, like Mondays, I had French first period. I wasn't going to pay any attention to him at all.

As soon as I sat down in class, I felt someone tap me on the shoulder. I knew it had to be Scott. He sat directly behind me. I just ignored it.

Listening to Monsieur DuBois's voice, I was able to forget who was sitting behind me. I forgot all about the carnation stem, at least until the class ended. Scott followed me out into the hallway, but I rushed into the bathroom to avoid him.

At lunchtime I steered Sandy to a table that had only two empty seats. That way Scott couldn't attempt to join us.

While we were eating, Sandy said, "They have hundreds of cats at the animal shelter in Jefferson and they're free, too."

Suddenly I got an idea. "Maybe we could

find a cat that looks just like Poughkeep-sie."

"That just might work," Sandy said. I remembered Aldo's face at the breakfast table. It sure would be nice to see him smile again.

"I'll ask my mother to take us to the animal shelter on Saturday," Sandy said. "I'm sure she'll do it. She and my father feel terrible about what happened."

"I won't tell Aldo," I said. "It will be a surprise."

And so on Saturday morning, Sandy and her mother and I drove to Jefferson to the animal shelter. Even before we got inside the building, we could hear the animals. There were cages and cages filled with dogs and cats. It didn't smell very good either.

There were lots of black cats with white patches, but I couldn't find one that looked exactly like Poughkeepsie. He had had a white spot on his head and two white legs. "At least we don't have to find a cat that looks like Peabody," I said. Peabody is quite unusual-looking. He has white spots all over his back that are the size of peas. That's how he got his name.

"That looks like a miniature Poughkeepsie," said Sandy.

"I can't bring home a kitten," I said. "Besides, it has white back legs and it was Poughkeepsie's front legs that were white."

"*Violà!*" I cried in front of a cage that held three grown cats.

Everyone in the area turned to look where I was pointing. I blushed. They probably thought I was one of those people who are crazy about animals.

"It looks exactly like Poughkeepsie," Sandy agreed as I carefully opened the cage and took out the cat.

"Come on Poughkeepsie," I said. "I'm taking you home."

Of course, I couldn't just walk out of the animal shelter. First I had to fill out a form. They didn't want to give me the cat because I was a minor. "My parents love cats," I told them. They still wouldn't have let me have the cat, but Mrs. Lorin signed the papers for me.

On the way back home, the cat sat on my lap. His claws clung to my jeans and scratched me through the denim. Instead of just walking through the door with him, I decided to sneak him into the house and let him loose. Maybe he would walk into Aldo's room and Aldo would be so thrilled to see him that he would pick him up and hug him. By the time he realized it wasn't the real Poughkeepsie, he would have already fallen in love with the new Poughkeepsie.

Sandy lent me a canvas tote bag, and I put the cat inside. "Call and tell me how it goes over," she said.

"Sure," I promised.

Upstairs in my room, I opened the tote bag and let the cat out. He walked around the room sniffing into every corner. I wondered if he could smell Peabody. The phone rang and I went to answer it.

"Hi," said Sandy. "How's it going?"

"Silly. I've only been in the house two minutes," I said.

"I know, but I can't wait to hear what happens. Can I come over?"

"*Oui*," I agreed. "But you have to act dumb. Don't let on that you know anything."

"Be right there," Sandy said and banged the receiver down.

She was at the door when I got there — that's how close her house is to mine. As I opened the door, we heard a howl from the top of the stairs.

It was Karen.

I ran up the stairs with Sandy behind me. Aldo appeared from his room, and my mother and father came running from the kitchen.

"What's the matter?" my mother asked.

"I've seen a ghost!" said Karen.

"You'd better explain," my father said.

"I was writing to my pen pal," Karen said, "telling him about how Poughkeepsie got killed. I looked up and there was the ghost of Poughkeepsie looking at me."

"It must have been Peabody," said Aldo.

"I've got eyes," said Karen. "This cat had white front feet. There's no way I could confuse the two cats."

"Oh, my goodness!" cried my mother,

pointing to the door of my room where the new cat was now standing. "It *is* Poughkeepsie."

For a moment, no one moved. Then Aldo leaped forward to grab the new cat. The cat ran into my room and under the bed. Aldo followed. The cat ran out and headed for the stairs. Everyone followed. Or at least my parents and Karen and Aldo followed. Sandy and I just stood there looking at each other.

Finally, after much chasing, some loud yowls from Peabody, and a few misses, the new cat was caught.

"It's a miracle, isn't it?" Sandy said to Aldo. "It's the reincarnation of Poughkeepsie."

"No, it's not," Aldo said firmly. "It's a nice cat and someone will want it, but not me."

"But it's exactly like Poughkeepsie," I said. "I thought you would be excited."

"It's a little like Poughkeepsie," said Aldo. "But it's not the same."

My father offered to drive me back to the animal shelter so I could return the cat.

"I'm afraid you acted too fast," he said. "It's that headstrong temperament of yours. Aldo isn't ready for a new cat."

Before we left, Aldo said, "I knew it couldn't be the ghost of Poughkeepsie."

"Smart boy," my father said. "There's no such thing as a ghost."

"That's not how I knew," said Aldo. "Poughkeepsie was a male cat. This one is a female."

7. Two Dates

When I got back from the animal shelter, my mother told me that I'd gotten a phone call while I was away.

"Sandy?" I asked.

"It was a boy."

"A boy? Why didn't you ask who it was?"

"He didn't leave his name," she said. "I told him to call after four o'clock."

I looked at my watch. It was ten minutes to four. I rushed upstairs, combed my hair, and put on some eye makeup. I knew whoever it was wouldn't be able to see me through the telephone, but I felt better anyhow.

At one minute after four the phone rang. "I'll get it," I screamed.

"Hello," I said. I could hardly get the word out of my mouth.

"Elaine? This is Scott."

"Scott?" I had gone out of my way to avoid him ever since the stem.

"From your French class at school."

As if I didn't know who he was!

"Listen," he said. "I've been trying to get up my nerve to call you all week. I feel just awful about that carnation stem you got. I paid for a flower, but it must have fallen off. I would never have sent you a stem."

I was so surprised that I didn't answer.

"Elaine? Are you still there?" Scott asked.

"Yes," I said, nodding my head vigorously.

"I hope you aren't angry anymore," he said.

I didn't know what to say. I had never spoken to Scott alone. Every time we talked before, Sandy was there.

"Listen. I was wondering," said Scott, "do you like thrillers?"

"Thrillers?"

"You know, scary movies. There's a new one that just opened at the triplex and I wonder if you would like to go tonight?"

"Oh," I gasped. "I'd love to." But even as I said it, I remembered that I was supposed to baby-sit.

"Great," said Scott.

"No, not great," I interrupted. "I just remembered I'm baby-sitting tonight. Unless, maybe my sister can take the job for me. Hold on and let me look for her."

I found Karen in the kitchen and asked her, but she already had a job. Sandy, I knew, was going out to dinner with her parents.

I ran back to the upstairs telephone and picked up the receiver.

"Hi, Scott," I said. "No dice. But maybe I can call the Kaufmanns and tell them that I'm sick."

"Hey, don't do that. Suppose they get another sitter and show up at the movie, too."

"Yikes," I said. "I never thought of that." Then I said, "How about going tomorrow?"

"I can't," said Scott. "My family has plans."

"Elaine," my mother called up the stairs. "Time's up."

I couldn't believe it. It was bad enough I couldn't go out with Scott. Now my mother wanted me to just hang up on him, too. I put my hand over the mouthpiece and shouted downstairs. "I can't hang up. *This is important.*"

"How about next Saturday?" Scott asked. "The movie should still be playing then."

"Yes, yes," I said happily. "I don't have any plans for next Saturday."

"Great," said Scott. "It's a date then."

"Elaine," my mother shouted again. She's wasting her time at our house. She should be working at a football stadium as a referee.

"Have fun baby-sitting," Scott said.

"Elaine." My mother shouted again.

"Listen, Scott," I said. "My mother is

expecting a phone call. I've got to hang up now."

"Okay," said Scott. "I'll see you in school. And don't forget we have a date next Saturday."

Forget? I didn't know how I was going to think about anything else for a whole week.

"Bye," I said.

I floated on air through the rest of the weekend. I was actually glad my date with Scott wasn't until next Saturday night because that gave me a whole week to anticipate it.

The only thing that kept my happiness from being complete was Aldo. He remained miserable and went around with a gloomy expression all the time. "Isn't there anything we can do to cheer him up?" I asked my mother. "I thought a new cat would make him happy."

"It's not that easy," my mother replied. "It takes time to recover from the loss of a loved one. Aldo was very attached to Poughkeepsie." As if I didn't know that already.

Feeling as happy as I did, I wanted everyone in the world to feel happy, too. So when Mrs. Kaufmann asked if I would be able to take her son Alexander to an animal show at the public library Friday after school, I thought of asking Aldo to come along. But I forgot about Aldo when Sandy called.

"If you marry Scott, then we'll be related," she told me. Sandy was busy playing matchmaker. She had given Scott my phone number.

"Who's getting married?" I said, glad that she couldn't see my red face. "He just asked me to go to the movies. I just think you are lucky to have such a cute cousin," I said. "All my cousins still suck their thumbs and wear diapers."

"Elaine!" my mother shouted up the stairs. "Time's up!"

For once I was actually relieved. I didn't want to talk too much about Scott. I wanted to think about it and keep my feelings to myself rather than share them with Sandy.

Sandy came down with a sore throat and

was absent from school on Wednesday. As I was walking out of French class, Monsieur DuBois called to me. He had never asked me to stay after class before. I thought he was going to congratulate me for getting an *A* on our last two assignments.

"Mademoiselle Sossi," he said. "I wish to speak with you for a moment. I have a personal question."

I looked up at his handsome face and thought I would faint. Suddenly it went through my head that he was going to ask me for a date.

"May I ask a favor of you?" he said.

"Sure." I could have kicked myself. I should have said, *"Oui."*

"I wonder if you are busy this coming Saturday?" he asked.

"No. No. I'm not busy," I said staring into his dark eyes. He *was* asking me for a date. In that moment, I forgot everything else in the world. All I could think of was Pierre.

A smile broke through his beard. "My

sister and her husband have come to visit," he said. "We would like to attend a concert in New York City on Saturday."

He wanted to take me to a concert! I began to go through my wardrobe. What would I wear? Would he expect me to call him Pierre?

"The problem is Garance."

"Garance?" I asked. I realized that I hadn't been listening. Was that his sister's name?

"She is *très petite*," he said.

His sister was very small?

"*Petite*?" I echoed stupidly.

"*Oui*. I wonder if you would be willing to take charge of Garance. Do you sometimes take care of little children? Baby-sitting, it is called here, *n'est pas*?"

I swallowed hard. *La petite* Garance was his niece. Monsieur DuBois was not asking me for a date at all. Or he was, but it wasn't exactly the sort of date I had in mind. For a moment, I was crushed. But then I thought, after all, there were a dozen other girls in my French class and it was *me* he was going to trust with his niece.

"I'd love to take care of her," I said, smiling.

"*Très bien*," said Monsieur DuBois. He wrote down his address on a slip of paper. "Could you come at *cinq heures*, five o'clock?" he asked.

"*Certainement*," I said.

I floated down the hall to my next class. But I sat down with a thud. How could I have forgotten? On Saturday night, I had a date with Scott.

8. A Big Mouth and Three Earrings

For once I knew what my father meant when he called me Hurricane Elaine. Why had I jumped so quickly to baby-sit for Monsieur DuBois? Well, it's hard to say no to someone when you are in love with them. And besides, I really had thought I was accepting a date with him when I said I was free Saturday. Somehow I had to tell either Scott or Monsieur DuBois that I wasn't really free on Saturday. Then I had a brainstorm. Maybe I could get Scott to change our date to Friday.

At lunch, he came and sat at my table. I was relieved that Sandy was absent so she couldn't hear what I said.

"Are you doing anything Friday night?" I asked Scott. When he said he was free, I would tell him I couldn't wait until Saturday for our date.

The only problem was that Scott said, "Bruce and Evan asked me to go bowling with them." He gave me his great friendly smile. I liked the way his blond hair fell into his eyes, too.

"I just can't wait till Saturday night for our date," I said sweetly. "I thought maybe we could go to the movie on Friday instead."

"Gosh," Scott said. "I don't want to wait either. But I did promise them." He looked tempted.

"It's less crowded at the movies on Friday," I suggested.

Scott nodded.

"So, how about it?"

"Gee, Elaine. I'd love to go with you on Friday, but it wouldn't be right to let Bruce and Evan down. They've been really nice to me since I moved here."

"Well, if they mean more to you than I do — "

"Hey, that's not fair," Scott protested.

I knew he was right, even as the words came out of my mouth.

The warning bell rang and I gathered up my books.

"We'll have a great time on Saturday," Scott promised. "It will be worth waiting for."

I didn't say anything. I didn't know what to say, so I just turned and walked off to my next class.

I couldn't wait until school was over. I didn't know what to do about Saturday. I wanted to help Monsieur DuBois. I didn't want some other girl in the class to take over for me. But I wanted to go out with Scott, too.

I decided to walk home from school to give myself time to think about what to do next. On the way I passed Gottlieb's Jewelry Shop. They were having a Mother's Day sale. It was almost May, and school would soon be over. Next year, I would be in high school. I wouldn't have Monsieur DuBois for French anymore. But maybe, now that I was baby-sitting for his niece, we would keep in touch. It would be awful if I never saw him again.

I noticed some earrings that were marked down to half price in the window. Next thing I knew I was inside the store. "If I bought those little star earrings that are on sale, would you make the extra holes in my ears for me?" I asked.

"Sure, no problem," said the woman behind the counter.

Within minutes, I had three earrings in my right ear instead of one. It looked great. I paid with the money I had put aside to give Monsieur DuBois on Friday, when he was going to collect for the French dinner. I figured I would ask my mother to lend me money until I earned some more.

I was so pleased with my new look I hardly thought about Saturday night.

"Good heavens," my mother gasped when I walked into the house. "What have you done?"

I never realized that her eyesight was so good. She spotted those tiny earrings from twenty feet away!

"I bought some new earrings," I explained.

"That's not all you did," said Karen, coming over to examine my ear more closely. "You've got two new holes to put the earrings into."

"What of it?" I said. "It's my money and my ear." I tried to act as if what I had done was the most natural thing in the world. But my parents had made a federal case out of letting me get my ears pierced the first time around. What was I in for now?

"I didn't give you permission," my mother said.

"I didn't know I needed permission," I said. "I'm not a baby."

"How many more holes are you going to get?" asked Aldo. "I think it looks nice," he added.

"See," I said. "Aldo thinks it looks nice."

"Well I don't," said my mother. "One hole in each ear was plenty. Next you'll be coming home with an earring in your nose."

"Don't you mean a nose ring in her nose?" asked Aldo.

Just then my father came in the door. "I forbid you to pierce your nose," he said. He dropped his briefcase and came over to inspect my ear.

"I never said I wanted to pierce my nose."

"You never said you wanted more holes in your ears, either," my mother pointed out.

"I didn't know I had to tell you everything that passed through my thoughts," I said. "I believe in intellectual freedom."

"This has nothing to do with intellectual freedom," my father said.

"Elaine wants another addition to the Bill of Rights," giggled Karen. "She wants Freedom of Speech, Freedom of the Press, and Freedom to Pierce."

As I started to protest, the telephone rang.

My father reached for the receiver and said, "Hello."

Saved by the bell, I thought. I started to walk away.

"Scott Welles?" said my father. "Hold on, I'll call Elaine."

I froze. I had temporarily forgotten about Scott and Saturday night.

"Tell me Scott," my father asked, "do you know the story of the three holes?"

Mon dieu! My father was going to tell Scott about how I had pierced my ears this afternoon. Then I heard my father say: "Well, well, well."

Karen and Aldo and my mother laughed at his corny joke. I ran to the upstairs extension. I did not need an audience when I spoke to Scott.

"Elaine. Are you mad at me?" Scott asked. He sounded unhappy.

"No. I just felt disappointed that we couldn't have our date on Friday."

"It's only three days until Saturday," said Scott.

"Yeah, but listen," I said. I took a deep breath. Better to say it and get it over with already. "I can't go out with you Saturday night. I promised someone I would babysit, and I don't know how I can get out of it."

"I thought you didn't have a job for this Saturday," said Scott.

"I know, but something came up. It's for Monsieur DuBois. He asked me to take care of his niece."

"Is that why he asked you to stay after class?"

"Yes," I admitted.

"Why didn't you tell him you were busy?"

How could I admit to Scott that I forgot we had a date? "I couldn't. After all, he's our teacher and everything."

"What's that got to do with anything? Saturday night belongs to you, not to him."

"Oh, Scott, you don't understand. I couldn't turn him down. He really needs me."

"I guess you need to work awfully hard to get your *A's*," said Scott.

"For your information, I am an *A* student, and it has nothing to do with babysitting. If you did your homework instead of going bowling, you'd have good grades, too, Scott Welles." I banged down the telephone.

After supper I tried to phone Sandy. She would understand why I couldn't turn down a chance to baby-sit for Monsieur DuBois. Mrs. Lorin answered the phone. She told me that Sandy's sore throat had gotten worse. She had taken some medicine and was fast asleep. There was no one I could talk to.

I was sitting on my bed feeling miserable when I heard a knock on my door. "Who's there?" I asked.

"It's me," said Aldo, coming inside.

"What do you want?" I asked. I didn't feel like sitting around and talking to him right now.

"I just wanted to tell you that you look pretty," he said. "I like your new earrings."

"Thanks a heap," I said.

"I really mean it," said Aldo sitting down beside me on the bed.

I looked at him. He looked as miserable as I felt. "Are you still thinking about Poughkeepsie?" I asked him.

He nodded. "It seems so lonely without him. He used to sleep on my bed and keep my toes warm at night."

Suddenly I remembered that I had something to tell him. "They are having an animal show at the library after school on Friday. I'm taking Alexander Kaufmann. Why don't you come with us? It's the kind of thing you'd like."

"What kind of animals?" asked Aldo.

"I don't know. It's called 'Mr. Happy and His Jolly Friends.' The friends are all animals. Come on. You'll have a good time."

"Okay," said Aldo, smiling at me.

"Great," I said. At least one of us was smiling.

9. Mr. Happy

The next day was totally rotten. I couldn't concentrate on my schoolwork. Scott and I avoided each other. Sandy was still absent. I had no one to listen to my side of the story.

At least Monsieur DuBois still liked me. He passed me in the hall and winked at me. At that moment, at least, I felt I had made the right decision. But later, in the lunchroom, when I saw Scott sitting at another table and laughing with some kids, I wished I was sitting next to him.

To make matters worse, Thursday night I had an argument with my mother. I asked her if I could borrow ten dollars to pay for the French class dinner.

"What's happened to all your baby-sitting money?" she wanted to know.

"I spent it," I admitted. "But I'll be earning more over the weekend. I can pay you back."

"Elaine," she said. "You have to learn how to budget your money. And you know I'm not very happy about what you did with your money yesterday." Of course that brought us back to my new earrings and the new holes in my ear. "You'll just have to tell your teacher that you can't give him the money until Monday." How embarrassing! Monsieur DuBois would be surprised and disappointed in me.

Finally, it was Friday afternoon and school was over for the week. I jumped off the school bus and raced home to drop off my books.

"Come on Aldo," I called. "We have to pick up Alexander and get to the library."

Alexander Kaufmann is four going on forty. He acts like he knows everything in the world already and can't wait to tell you about it. He was probably born speaking full sentences. I bet he's going to be a teacher when he grows up.

The library room was already filled with small children and their parents when we arrived. I was afraid Aldo would be sorry he had agreed to come with me. I was at least being paid to attend. But as soon as Mr. Happy appeared on the stage with his Jolly Friends, I knew my idea had been a good one. The Jolly Friends were three trained dogs. Aldo couldn't take his eyes off them. They wore ruffled collars and stood on little step stools.

"George. Come here," Mr. Happy called.

One of the dogs jumped down from his stool. The children squealed with delight. Aldo gave a small cheer for the clever dog, too.

Alexander pulled at my sleeve. "He must be named after George Washington," he told me. "Did you know that George Washington was the first president of the United States?"

I caught Aldo's eye and smiled. "As a matter of fact, Alexander, I believe I did hear that somewhere before."

Aldo grinned at me and then turned to watch George leap through a hoop, climb a ladder, and jump off a diving board into Mr. Happy's arms. Everyone laughed and applauded — except Alexander, who took this opportunity to tell me that dogs did not need to be taught how to swim. If you threw a dog into the water, he would begin to swim instinctively.

"All right, Helen. Now it's your turn," called Mr. Happy.

"Cockerpoo!" shouted Alexander as a small dog with curly brown hair, wearing a pink ruffled collar and a pink bow on her head, jumped down off the stool.

"*Shhhh*," I said to Alexander.

"Cockerpoo!" he called out again.

"Alexander," I said sharply. "I'm going to tell your mother to wash your mouth out with soap."

"Here's Helen!" Mr. Happy called out. "And you are absolutely correct, young man. Helen is a cockerpoo. She is part cocker spaniel and part poodle."

Helen danced around the stage. Alexander looked at me and said, "Helen of

Troy was the most beautiful woman in the world. Did you know that?"

I didn't, and I didn't know how a kid of four did, either.

After Helen did her doggy tricks, Mr. Happy called on Einstein.

"I know who Einstein was," I said before Alexander could launch into a lecture on the famous scientist.

Mr. Happy explained to the audience that Einstein was good at arithmetic. He then put out signs around the stage with numbers from one to ten written on them. "Now I'm going to ask Einstein some arithmetic questions," Mr. Happy announced. "Let's see if he can get the answers. How much is four plus five?"

The shaggy white dog ran around the stage and grabbed the sign with the number nine.

"Nine!" called out Alexander. He had been counting on his fingers.

"All right," Mr. Happy said. "Here's a hard one. How much is four times two?"

Alexander added with his fingers. Two and two and two and two. By the time he figured out that the answer was eight, Einstein had already circled the stage with the correct number in his mouth.

"Wow!" said Aldo. "I wonder how he learned to do arithmetic?"

"Do you think that dog is smarter than me?" Alexander asked.

"I think he is a very smart dog, and you are a very smart boy," I said.

Alexander smiled, satisfied with my answer.

When the program ended, we joined the rest of the audience up at the stage. Everyone wanted to pet the dogs. "Maybe I can get a dog," said Alexander.

"That would be nice," I said. This little kid really needed a chance to play and be like other kids. He already had enough information crammed into his brain to get him through high school.

"Do you like dogs?" Alexander asked Aldo.

Aldo turned to him. "I sure do," he said. "Mr. Happy gave me this card with his name on it." Aldo turned to me. "I told him that I want to be a vet when I grow up."

I decided then and there that Aldo should get a dog — and fast. He had enjoyed the show a lot. It was the first time I had seen him looking happy since Poughkeepsie was killed.

10. Chez DuBois

I earned three dollars on Friday afternoon and even better, I had the satisfaction of seeing Aldo smile for a change. Now I still had to get through Saturday until it was time to go to Monsieur DuBois's house. I was excited but I was nervous, too. In class I called him Monsieur DuBois. Should I call him Pierre at home?

It was arranged that my father would drive me over and that Monsieur DuBois would drive me home. I would be alone with him in his car. My heart raced at the thought.

My father waited in the car until I rang Monsieur DuBois's doorbell. I wished he would just leave so I didn't look like a baby. I wanted Pierre to think of me as a woman, not a kid.

The door opened, and a woman was standing there.

"You must be Elaine," she said, smiling at me. "Come in, dear."

Monsieur DuBois's sister looked like a movie star. She had blond hair and a great figure, and she wore exotic perfume and lots of eye makeup. She didn't look much like her brother.

"I'm Genevieve DuBois," she said. "My husband has told me what a good student you are."

I swallowed hard. This woman was Pierre's *wife*. Even in my best jeans, I felt like a slob next to her. How could I have ever dreamed that Monsieur DuBois would fall in love with me? Why hadn't it occurred to me that he might be married?

"And here is Garance," she said.

I looked at a little girl of about three who was looking at me suspiciously.

"What an unusual name," I said.

"Garance is French for a wildflower,"

Monsieur DuBois said. He had on a dark turtleneck sweater and he looked even more handsome than he did at school. I smiled at him and then remembered that he was a married man.

I was introduced to Garance's parents. Then Mrs. DuBois said something to her husband in French. She spoke so rapidly that I couldn't catch it. He answered her, and again I couldn't follow it. The French he spoke in class was quite different from the French he spoke at home. Every once in a while I caught a single word and recognized it. It was really frustrating. I was an *A* student, and here I could hardly understand a word they were saying. Garance had put her thumb in her mouth. It occurred to me that although I couldn't follow the conversation, this little kid could. That really made me feel stupid.

"What are you going to hear?" I asked Monsieur DuBois.

"Mahler," he replied, smiling.

"I never heard him," I said. "Does he play an instrument or sing?"

"Mahler was an Austrian composer,"

Mrs. DuBois told me. "He lived at the turn of the century."

"Oh." I really felt like an idiot. I was better off when they were speaking in French. Then, at least, I couldn't make stupid comments.

I was shown the room where Garance was to sleep and told that her bedtime was eight o'clock.

"Okay," I said.

It wasn't okay, but it was too late for me to do anything about it. I watched Monsieur DuBois help his wife adjust the stole she was wearing around her shoulders. Garance's mother bent down and kissed her daughter.

"*Au revoir,*" the adults called to us as they got into Monsieur DuBois's car.

Garance and I stood watching silently as the car started off. I felt abandoned. Why was I here with this little girl? I could have been at home getting ready for my date with Scott. Now Scott wasn't even talking to me. I wondered if he was taking someone else to the movie. I realized now that to Monsieur DuBois I was just another student, a ninth-grade kid. At least to Scott, I was someone special — that is, I used to be someone special. Now I was nothing.

Garance took her thumb out of her mouth, and as if she had unplugged a bottle, a loud howl poured out. It was an American howl. I didn't need a translation to understand it.

"Hey, Garance. We're going to have a good time together," I said. She knew I was lying and continued screaming. She didn't want to stay with me anymore than I wanted to stay with her.

I was afraid the neighbors would think I was torturing her, so I quickly pushed her inside the door and shut it tightly behind us.

"Don't cry. Don't cry," I said. "Your parents will be back soon."

"*Maman, maman*," she screamed.

"*Sois sage*," I said, remembering an expression that we had learned in class. It means "be calm."

"*Maman, maman*," Garance continued yelling. I groaned to myself. Garance might be French, but she was no different from any other little boy or girl in Woodside, New Jersey who had been left with a strange new baby-sitter. I would have to do something, or she would keep on crying for a long time.

I sat down on the floor and put my arms around her. She pulled away. She did not want to be hugged by me.

"Look, Garance," I said. I went over to the television set and turned it on, hoping that the pictures on the screen would soothe her. They did not.

"*Non, non, non,*" she cried.

I went into the kitchen and found a box of cookies on top of the counter. "Would you like one?" I offered.

"*Non, non,*" she howled at me.

I put the cookie in my own mouth and chewed on it without even tasting it. I knew all the French words for eating in a restaurant or asking for a room in a hotel but I didn't know any of the things that a mother would say to comfort a crying child. I tried to remember the songs we had learned in class. Somehow I didn't think "La Marseillaise" would be effective. Would an American child stop crying if she heard the "Star Spangled Banner"?

I had been left with crying children dozens of times. They always get tired of crying if you wait long enough. You just have to keep calm yourself. But that evening, I didn't feel at all calm. Instead I began to feel like crying myself.

"*Maman, maman,*" sniffed Garance. And before I knew it, I was crying too. Why had I broken my date with Scott? Where was Scott now? I felt in my pocket for a tissue as the tears sprang out of my eyes. I sat down on the sofa and began to sob. This was the worst evening of my life.

I guess my crying must have surprised Garance because she stopped her howling. She came over to me and began to stroke my arm. That little three-year-old child was trying to make *me* stop crying. That made me feel sadder than ever. I put my arms around her, and we hugged each other as my tears dripped onto her head.

Eventually, we both stopped crying. I found a tissue and blew my nose and found another and mopped up Garance's tears, too. Then I heated the chicken and vegetables that had been left for us in the kitchen. Neither of us ate much. After supper, I helped Garance unbutton her dress and put on her nightgown. I couldn't read to her or do any of the games I usually played with the children I baby-sat for. It didn't matter. Garance put her thumb in her mouth, and she was ready to sleep. I tucked her into bed and kissed her. It wasn't her fault that my evening — in fact my whole life — had been ruined because I had impulsively agreed to spend the evening here.

I went into the living room and looked at the books on the shelves. They were mostly in French, but when I opened one and tried to read it, I couldn't understand more than a couple of words. So much for being an *A* student.

I turned on the television. I would watch an old film. In English. At least that wouldn't be too hard on my brain. About halfway through the movie, the door bell rang. I've been warned hundreds of times not to open the door when I am baby-sitting, but I peeked through a little window by the door to see who was there. To my amazement, it was Scott. I was so surprised that I opened the door before I even thought how ghastly I must look. My mascara was smudged all over and my eyes were still red from crying. But at that moment I forgot everything.

"What are you doing here?" I asked him.

"I thought I could give you a hand," he said, smiling.

"Didn't you go to the movie?" I asked.

"I can go another time," he said. "Aren't you going to ask me to come in?"

"I can't," I said. "I shouldn't even have opened the door. I'm not supposed to let people in when I baby-sit."

"But I'm not just *anybody*," Scott protested. "And besides, I had to work really hard to find you. Do you realize how many families named DuBois there are in this town? I've been going all over Woodside ringing the wrong door bells. I thought you'd be glad to see me."

"Well I am glad. But that doesn't mean I can let you in," I said.

"The least you can do is let me come in for a glass of water," Scott said. "I won't stay."

"Okay," I agreed. "But you have to leave right away. I don't want Monsieur DuBois to find you here. He won't think I'm a very reliable baby-sitter if he sees me entertaining my friends in his house."

"Stop worrying," said Scott. "I'll go in a minute."

Scott was still drinking his glass of water when Monsieur DuBois returned.

"Elaine," he said, looking very upset. "Is this the way you take care of Garance?"

"She's fast asleep," I said. "I didn't think you would mind Scott being here. After all, he's in your class, too."

Monsieur DuBois shook his head disapprovingly. "I am very disappointed," he said. "In two weeks we will have our dinner party. That is the time for everyone to celebrate together. There is no reason for Scott to be here this evening. Of all my students, I was confident that I could trust you."

"Well, gosh," said Scott, looking as embarrassed as I felt. "It's my fault," he said. "I just invited myself in."

Mrs. DuBois and Garance's mother began to speak in French. *"Oui, oui,"* Monsieur DuBois said. I wondered what they were saying.

"My wife reminds me that we were young once, too," he said. He opened his wallet and counted out the bills to pay me.

"Garance is a very sweet child," I said. "I'm sorry if I let you down."

"What's done is done," said Mrs. DuBois. "Take the children home," she told her husband. "It is late, and they are tired."

Scott and I squeezed into the front seat with Monsieur DuBois. We felt like naughty children who had just been scolded. Monsieur DuBois dropped me off at my house and then drove off to take Scott home.

As I got ready for bed, I took the money I had earned out of the pocket of my jeans. At least, now I had enough to pay for the dinner at the French restaurant. On Monday, I would pay it back to Monsieur DuBois.

11. Einstein's Daughter

Aldo's birthday was on Saturday, May 17th, and that was also the date of the French dinner Monsieur DuBois had arranged for our class.

Sandy had recovered from her sore throat, and I had told her about what happened when I baby-sat for Monsieur DuBois's niece. I was still so embarrassed I could hardly bear to sit in his class. When we passed in the hallway at school, Scott nodded but kept going. He seemed just as embarrassed as I was about how the evening at Monsieur DuBois's had turned out. I was not looking forward to the dinner, despite Sandy's attempts to reassure me.

Aldo had said that he didn't want a party for his birthday. He was still mourning Poughkeepsie. Karen thought we should make him a surprise party, but my mother said we should respect Aldo's wish for a quiet celebration. It didn't look like May 17th was going to be a very happy day at our house — unless I had a surprise for Aldo. And that's what I planned to do. I would get Aldo a dog for his birthday. I just knew he would really love one.

I tried the idea out on Sandy, who had some misgivings, but agreed to check it out with her parents. Her father offered to drive us to the Jefferson animal shelter first thing Saturday morning if I was certain it was all right. Of course I was certain. It wouldn't be like the time with the cat, I promised him. "You should have seen Aldo at the dog show at the library. He loved it and I know he will love having a dog of his own."

The days passed slowly. At least the weather was great. It reminded me that there were just a few weeks left of the school year. Next year Sandy and I would be going to high school. Scott would be at the high school, too.

After so many days of beautiful weather, it was too bad that it had to be raining on the morning of Aldo's birthday. I crossed my fingers that it would stop before the evening. It would be awful if I had to wear rain boots to the restaurant. I thought Aldo would be disappointed in the weather, but he didn't even seem to notice the rain. He didn't seem surprised that there was only one wrapped package waiting for him on the kitchen table. It was from my Aunt Eleanor and Uncle Thomas.

"I'll have a present for you at lunchtime," I promised.

"My gift will be here later, too," said Karen.

"It looks like a big afternoon is in store for you," said my mother. She leaned down and gave Aldo a kiss. "Your father and I will also have your gift this afternoon."

Aldo took all this in without a complaint. *I* would have been annoyed, after waiting a whole year for my birthday, if there weren't more presents waiting for me.

Aldo just smiled and said, "I'm getting myself a birthday present, too. Wait till you see it."

I finished breakfast quickly and put on my rain slicker and boots. My family thought I was going to the flea market with Sandy. I didn't lie. I just said we were going to Jefferson and let them draw their own conclusions.

Mr. Lorin drove us to the animal shelter. "You're certain this is all right with everyone at your house?" he asked me twice as we drove along.

The three of us walked around the shelter. There were so many dogs, it wasn't easy to choose one. How could I tell which dog had a high I.Q. like Mr. Happy's Einstein? Finally, I picked a little brown-and-white dog that licked my hand when I petted him through the mesh of his cage.

Mr. Lorin signed the papers for me, and we all got back into the car.

"I can't wait to see Aldo's face," I said. "This is going to be the best birthday present he ever got."

Mr. Lorin dropped me off at my door.

I jumped out of the car with the little dog nestled underneath my slicker so he wouldn't get wet. No one answered when I rang the bell, so I had to dig into my handbag to find my key. It was pretty tricky to do that with a dog under my coat!

I intended to whip off my coat and surprise Aldo with the dog. The problem was that neither Aldo nor my parents nor Karen was at home. I was alone with the dog. I decided to hide him in my bedroom. The dog had been very quiet up until now, but when I shut him inside my room, he began to whine. I went down to the kitchen to see if there was something in the refrigerator he could eat. The birthday cake Karen had made was on the kitchen table. It looked delicious! I snitched some frosting from one corner where it wouldn't show. Yummy!

I wasn't sure what to feed the dog so I just turned on the radio to cover the noise he was making. I found some good music and lay down on the living-room rug to exercise. I had done a few stretches when the phone rang.

"What's happening?" asked Sandy.

"*Rien.* Nothing. No one's home." I said. Those were my famous last words because even as I said them I heard someone at the door. It was Karen and she was holding a carton. It was shaking in her arms and a muffled sound was coming from it. I dropped the telephone. Inside the carton was a dog.

"Isn't it darling?" asked Karen.

"How could you?" I demanded.

"I know you hate animals," said Karen. "But Aldo *needs* a dog. I saw a sign offering to give a puppy away. It just seemed meant for Aldo."

Just then, the door opened again and my parents came in. My mother was holding a puppy in her arms.

"Look what we got for Aldo," she said. Her eyes widened as she saw the carton that Karen had put on the floor.

Before I could say a thing, the doorbell rang. "Maybe it's another dog," said my mother, laughing.

It wasn't a dog. It was Sandy. "I think we got disconnected," she said.

The telephone receiver was hanging where I had dropped it when Karen came home. "I forgot all about you," I said.

Sandy stood staring at the puppies. "Wait a minute," she said. "That's not the one that you . . ."

Her words were lost in the confusion of the door opening again. Aldo came in wearing his rain poncho. From underneath its folds, he pulled out another dog.

"This is like a circus act," my father said.

"I got her from Mr. Happy," said Aldo. "She's the daughter of Einstein."

"Einstein's daughter?" my mother asked. She was totally confused.

Aldo put the dog on the floor and the other puppies began to sniff at it. Then one of the dogs began yapping, and the other two started in, too.

"Well, we can't all stand here dripping wet," my father said. He took off his raincoat and took my mother's from her. Karen and Sandy and Aldo took off their raincoats, too. The three puppies frisked together on the living-room floor.

"I didn't know you were going to get me a dog, so I got one for myself," said Aldo. "It's my birthday so I didn't think you would get angry."

"I'm not angry," said my mother, "just surprised."

"This certainly is a surprising situation," my father said.

"It's not over yet," said Sandy.

"Well, you see . . ." I began. But then the doorbell rang.

It was Aldo's friend DeDe, holding you know what in her arms.

"Happy birthday, Aldo," she said as she thrust a puppy into his arms.

Now there were four dogs barking and running around in the living room.

"Will someone please shut off that radio," my father begged, sinking down on the sofa.

"What could be more surprising than this?" my mother asked.

I turned off the radio. I knew the answer to my mother's question. Five dogs. Five dogs *are* more surprising than four.

As soon as the music was off, everyone

could hear the yipping of the puppy that was locked in my room.

"What's that?" Aldo asked.

"That's your birthday present," I said. Suddenly I couldn't stop laughing. It was just so funny.

Aldo ran upstairs to get it and came back cuddling the puppy in his arms. "Can I keep them all?" asked Aldo. He was probably already imagining his trained dog act: Master Aldo and His Noisy Friends.

"You'll have to make a choice," my father said. "One dog is enough for any family."

"We had two cats," I said. What was I saying? Why do I always talk before I think? I didn't want to remind Aldo that we didn't have two cats any longer.

"Hey, where's Peabody?" asked Karen.

Aldo and DeDe went off in search of the cat. They found him hiding under the bed in Aldo's room.

"This is one time when we all went tearing around like hurricanes," my father said. "And the result is a house full of dogs."

"How about some lunch for everyone?" my mother offered. "And don't we have to feed all these dogs, too?"

"I brought some dog food," offered DeDe. Sure enough, she had a couple of cans in the pockets of her raincoat.

So the puppies all ate canned puppy food and the rest of us had vegetarian lasagna, which is Aldo's favorite meal. For dessert we had the cake that Karen had baked. The puppies sat underfoot sniffing at all the guests, and Aldo had a party after all. Only Peabody didn't attend. He was still hiding under the bed upstairs.

"This is the first party I ever went to where there were almost as many dogs as people," said DeDe. "My dog Cookie is going to be very upset when she hears she didn't get invited."

"Oh, please don't tell her," said Aldo. He said it so seriously that we all had to laugh.

"This doesn't mean that I don't miss Poughkeepsie," Aldo said. Einstein's daughter was curled up on his lap.

"Of course not," said my father. "One

thing has nothing to do with the other."

"Which dog are you going to keep?" asked DeDe.

Aldo looked down at Einstein's daughter. She was his first choice. He had chosen her himself. But he wasn't happy about having to give up the others.

"I guess my mother wouldn't let me keep so many dogs either," DeDe admitted. "But it's too bad this little pup isn't going to have a new home here."

"I've got an idea," I said. "I'm going to take a dog over to Alexander Kaufmann's house. That kid ought to own a dog."

"I've a better idea," my father said. "Phone and speak with his parents about it. You don't want to disappoint Alexander if his parents don't agree to your plan."

My father was right, I knew. But as it turned out, Mr. and Mrs. Kaufmann agreed to let me bring a puppy to their house.

Then Karen thought of giving a puppy to Keith Collins, who is a little kid that she baby-sits for. Mr. Collins said he had always wanted a dog, and so he agreed, too.

"Two down and two to go," my father said.

"Maybe I can convince my parents to let me keep this one," said Sandy. She was cuddling the little brown-and-white puppy that we had brought from the animal shelter. "I'm going to go and ask them." She took the puppy with her. I wondered what her father would say when he heard we weren't going to keep it after all.

"Three down and one to go," my father said as the door banged behind Sandy.

"Maybe Sandy's parents won't let her keep the dog," said Karen.

"If I know Ed Lorin," my father laughed, "that dog is hers."

Aldo picked up the puppy my parents had brought him. "Couldn't he stay for the night?" he begged.

"Oh, Aldo," my mother sighed. "Two dogs . . ."

I had a feeling that we were going to keep two dogs after all. And the funny thing is, much as I've always disliked animals, it didn't bother me at all.

12. A Happy Beginning

The rain stopped, and with all the dogs plus the dogs being delivered to their new homes, the afternoon passed very quickly. Before I knew it, it was time to get ready for the evening.

Sandy phoned me twice while I was dressing. Once she wanted to know if I was wearing blue or green eye shadow. The other time she wanted to know what I was wearing over my dress.

"My mother is lending me a stole," I said.

"A fur stole!" Sandy gasped.

"Not fur, silly. Aldo would disown me. It's amazing I can get away with leather shoes. It's a woolen stole from Mexico. It's bright red and my mother got it for Christmas last year." I didn't tell Sandy I'd seen Mrs. DuBois wearing a woolen stole when she went to the concert.

My mother had been very nice about letting me borrow the stole. And she didn't even get angry when the phone rang for me almost as soon as I hung up. It was Sandy again.

"I forgot to ask how long you thought it would take us to walk to the restaurant."

"Ten minutes," I guessed.

"That's what I thought, too," said Sandy. "Okay. Ring my bell. I'll be waiting."

Long before seven I was all dressed and ready. My family was sitting around the table eating supper. It felt funny not to be with them. But maybe now that I was almost in high school, things were going to be different.

"You look great!" said Aldo when I went downstairs.

"Yes," my mother agreed. "Even with all those earrings, you look lovely."

Einstein's daughter poked her head out from under the table. I don't know about her arithmetic, but she is clever. There is bound to be food dropping off the table. Of course, she doesn't know yet that my brother is a vegetarian.

"Save me another piece of birthday cake," I said as I waved good-bye.

Le Petit Bistro really is small. The owner is a friend of Monsieur DuBois, and he had closed the restaurant so that only our French class was there that evening. I had never seen everyone all dressed up before. When Sandy and I arrived, there were two huddles of kids. Girls on one side, boys on the other. Almost every guy in the class was wearing a necktie. I could hardly recognize Scott. His hair was slicked down with gel or something, instead of falling into his eyes as it usually did. When he grinned, I saw his dimple.

The girls in our class all looked great, too. And standing there with Sandy, I realized what a special thing this dinner was. Our school makes no fuss about finishing junior high. There is no graduation ceremony, no prom, no school assembly like some schools have. You finish your last class in junior high, and ten weeks later you begin high school. This evening was like a graduation party.

Monsieur DuBois introduced his wife to everyone. Now that I knew he was married, I wasn't jealous. In fact, I was glad that I already knew her.

All the tables in the restaurant had been pushed together to form one very long one. The boys crowded together along one side, but Monsieur DuBois said, "In France, ladies and gentlemen do not sit separately."

"Come on Elaine," Scott said, "you promised that you would let me sit next to you."

"Don't forget that we have to speak only in French."

"*Shhh.* Don't remind him," said Evan.

I wondered if anyone would try and get away with whispering in English. But everyone took the occasion very seriously.

We inquired politely about everyone's health. That was in one of the first lessons in our book.

Two waiters distributed menus. We had a choice of *coq au vin*, which is chicken cooked in wine, or *boeuf en daube*. That's beef cooked with wine. I knew Karen would want to hear all about this. My mother didn't let her cook with alcohol yet.

Sandy and I did most of the talking at our end of the table. After all, we were both *A* students. Evan and Scott said *merci* whenever we passed the salt and pepper and not much more than that. Still it was fun pretending to be sophisticated diners. Monsieur DuBois and his wife walked around and spoke with everyone, too. There were many conversations about the rain this morning and the absence of rain now. We all talked about whether the food was good or not good. Everyone, even those who didn't like French, liked the the food. For dessert there was a big cake *Un gâteau*. It was good, but not better than Karen's.

When we finished eating, Mrs. DuBois led the class in singing French songs. I didn't feel that sophisticated diners would end their meal that way. But after a minute or two, I joined in with the others. Mrs. DuBois taught us a couple of new songs. She has a nice voice.

At ten o'clock, the waiters dimmed the lights. A few parents were waiting outside to take their children home. I was glad that my parents had not insisted on picking Sandy and me up.

"English!" said Scott, as we walked out into the street. "I never knew how good it could feel to speak my own language."

"You were very quiet all evening," Sandy needled him. Scott and Evan were walking with us.

"You would be, too, if you only knew a dozen words of a language."

"You could have counted to ten," I laughed.

"There's no point in talking just to hear your own voice," said Scott. We all laughed.

Even though we walked slowly through the warm May evening, we arrived at our street too soon. I wondered if Evan and

Sandy would come to my door with Scott. They didn't. Evan walked off toward Sandy's house, and Scott walked with me. He sat down on the steps in front of my house, and I sat down beside him.

This was one crazy day, I thought. I hadn't expected it to end with Scott and me sitting side by side, first at dinner and now here. Scott leaned toward me. "Are you warm enough?"

"*Hmmm*," I agreed. The wool stole around my shoulders and Scott's arm around the wool stole were perfect.

Scott leaned closer still. "You were the prettiest girl at the restaurant," he said.

"Too bad you couldn't say that in French."

"Some things you don't need any language to say," Scott whispered. I felt his breath against my cheek.

My father complains about how dim the streetlights are in our neighborhood, but at that moment, I was glad it was so dark. Scott moved his face next to mine and his lips brushed my cheek. I moved my head toward him, and Scott's nose landed in my eye. That never happens in the movies.

But then Scott's lips found mine and neither his nose nor mine was in the wrong place. His lips felt so warm that I suddenly thought how nice it was that he didn't have a moustache or a beard. I would hate kissing anyone with all that hair. I'd probably get hair in my mouth and it would be awful.

Finally, I pulled away to catch my breath.

Scott jumped up from the step. He went over to the tulips that were growing along the walk and pulled one up. I knew my mother wouldn't like that. But before I could tell Scott to stop, he came back and held the flower out to me. "I owe you a flower," he said, and made a mock bow.

"I don't think a flower picked from my own yard counts," I said, but I took it anyhow and stuck it in my hair.

"Let's try not to fight again," said Scott.

"I promise," I said. "But I have to warn you. My father calls me Hurricane Elaine."

"I'm really glad my family moved to

Woodside this spring," Scott said. "Sandy told me about you."

"What did she say?"

"She said you didn't know how to play tennis. So I'm going to teach you this summer. I'm much better at tennis than French," he added.

That wasn't what I wanted to hear. But it would be fun to learn how to play tennis with Scott as my teacher.

"And you can coach me in French so I won't be so stupid when I get to high school," he added.

"It's a deal," I said. Despite myself, a yawn escaped from me.

"Boring you?" Scott teased.

"I'm not bored," I said. "It's just that I got up very early this morning."

"Me, too," said Scott. He helped me up from the step and put his arms around me again. "Its time to say good night. But I'll talk to you tomorrow." I watched him walk down the street until I couldn't see him any longer before I went into the house.

I was glad that my parents were not downstairs. I didn't want to talk to anyone now. I turned off the light and tiptoed up the stairs to my room. I didn't see the puppies anywhere. I guess they were sleeping in Aldo's room.

Peabody was asleep on my bed. He probably felt safer away from the newest members of the Sossi family.

I filled the toothbrush mug with water and put my tulip in it. I would press it and save it forever.

I slipped my nightgown on over my head and got into bed carefully, so as not to disturb Peabody. The cat stretched and yawned and then settled back down at the foot of my bed. I was feeling so good that I never even thought about fleas.

About the Author

JOHANNA HURWITZ grew up in New York and received degrees from Queens College and Columbia University. She has worked as a children's librarian in school and public libraries in both New York City and Long Island. She is the author of *Aldo Applesauce*, *DeDe Takes Charge!* and *Tough-Luck Karen*, among many other books. Ms. Hurwitz and her family live in Great Neck, New York.